Two-Minute Fairy Tales

Adapted by MARY PACKARD • Illustrated by ANN SCHWENINGER

A GOLDEN BOOK • NEW YORK
Western Publishing Company, Inc., Racine, Wisconsin 53404

Jack and the Beanstalk

Once upon a time there was a boy named Jack who lived with his mother in a tiny cottage. Many years before, an evil giant had stolen Jack's father's fortune, and now they were very poor.

One day Jack's mother said to him, "Son, you must take your cow to market and sell her so we may buy food." Jack set out at once.

On his way to the market Jack met an old man. "I'll trade you these magic beans for your cow," said the old man. Jack agreed to the trade. But when he returned home and showed his mother the beans, she was very angry.

"Now we shall starve!" she cried as she threw the beans out the window.

The next morning Jack looked out his window. A tremendously tall beanstalk seemed to reach up to the sky.

"Those *were* magic beans!" shouted Jack. He ran outside and quickly climbed the beanstalk.

At the top of the beanstalk was a beautiful castle. Jack hopped up to the open window and perched on the sill. He saw a huge giant sitting at a table, staring at a little hen.

"Lay, hen, lay!" roared the giant, and the hen laid a golden egg.

"Very good," said the giant with a yawn. Soon he fell fast asleep.

"That's my father's golden hen!" thought Jack. When the giant began snoring, Jack jumped through the window, snatched up the hen, and quickly slid down the beanstalk.

"Oh, Jack," said his mother happily, "you have found your father's hen!"

The next day Jack climbed the beanstalk again. And once again he peeked into the giant's castle. This time the giant was listening to a golden harp.

"Play, harp, play!" commanded the giant. And the harp played such beautiful music that it soon lulled the giant to sleep. Jack jumped through the window, seized the harp, and quickly slid down the beanstalk.

"Oh, Jack!" said his mother. "You have found your father's golden harp!"

The next morning Jack climbed the beanstalk again. The giant was in a terrible mood because he had just discovered that his hen and his harp were missing. He sniffed the air and said,

"Fee, fi, fo, fum.
I smell the blood of an Englishman.
Be he alive or be he dead,
I'll grind his bones to make my bread.

3.

"Wife!" growled the giant. "Fetch me my gold. That will surely cheer me up."

The giant's wife hurried to obey him. The giant counted his gold pieces for a while, and then he closed his eyes. When Jack thought the giant had fallen asleep, he jumped through the window.

But the giant had only been pretending to sleep, and he leapt up with a roar. "I knew I smelled boy!" he bellowed as he raced after Jack.

"Mother, get the ax ready!" Jack shouted from the top of the beanstalk.

As Jack climbed down, the beanstalk began to sway. Jack looked up and saw that the giant was coming down, too. Jack dropped the gold and slid all the way down to the ground. Then he took the ax and cut the beanstalk in two. There was a great crash, and the giant fell through the ground, all the way to the center of the earth.

Jack and his mother lived happily ever after. For who could be sad with a hen to lay golden eggs, a harp that plays beautiful music, and gold to buy all your heart desires?

The Three Bears

Once upon a time there were three bears—a great big father bear, a middle-sized mother bear, and a little baby bear.

They lived in a house in the forest. Every morning the three bears went for a walk while their porridge cooled.

One day a little girl called Goldilocks went for a walk in the forest. She came to the house of the three bears.

Goldilocks knocked at the door, but there was no answer. She walked into the house and saw three chairs. She sat in Father Bear's great big chair. It was much too hard.

She sat in Mother Bear's middle-sized chair. It was much too soft.

She sat in Baby Bear's little chair. It was just right, but the little chair broke!

Then Goldilocks tasted the porridge in Father Bear's great big bowl. It was too hot.

She tasted the porridge in Mother Bear's middle-sized bowl. It was too cold.

She tasted the porridge in Baby Bear's little bowl. It was just right, and Goldilocks ate it all up.

Then Goldilocks decided to go upstairs and take a nap. She tried Father Bear's great big bed. It was too hard.

She tried Mother Bear's middle-sized bed. It was too soft.

She tried Baby Bear's little bed. It was just right, and Goldilocks lay down and fell fast asleep.

Then the three bears came home. "Someone has been sitting in my chair!" roared Father Bear.

"Someone has been sitting in my chair!" said Mother Bear.

"Someone has been sitting in my chair!" squeaked Baby Bear. "And now it's broken!"

"Someone has been tasting my porridge!" roared Father Bear.

"Someone has been tasting my porridge!" said Mother Bear.

"Someone has been tasting my porridge!" squeaked Baby Bear. "And someone has eaten it all up!"

Then up the stairs they went. "Someone has been lying in my bed!" roared Father Bear.

"Someone has been lying in my bed!" said Mother Bear.

"Someone has been lying in my bed!" squeaked Baby Bear. "And she's still there!"

Then Goldilocks woke up and saw the three bears. She was so frightened that she jumped right up and ran down the stairs, out of the house, and into the forest. And Goldilocks never went back to that little house again!

The Three Little Pigs

Once upon a time three little pigs went out into the world to seek their fortunes. The first thing each of them had to do was build a house. The first little pig built a house of straw.

The little pig was just settling in when a big bad wolf knocked at the door and said, "Little pig, little pig, let me come in!"

"Not by the hair of my chinny-chin-chin!" said the first little pig.

Then the wolf huffed, and he puffed, and he blew the house in.

The little pig escaped just in time to the house of the second little pig. He was building a house of sticks. Just as he was finishing it, the big bad wolf knocked at the door and said, "Little pig, little pig, let me come in!"

"Not by the hair of our chinny-chin-chins!" said the second little pig and his brother.

Then the big bad wolf huffed, and he puffed, and he blew the house in. The little pigs got out just in time and ran to the house of the third little pig.

Now, the third little pig was building a house of bricks. It was much more difficult to build than a straw house or a house of sticks.

The little pig had just gotten the last brick in place when the big bad wolf knocked at the door and said, "Little pig, little pig, let me come in!"

"Not by the hair of our chinny-chin-chins!" said the three little pigs.

Then the big bad wolf huffed, and he puffed, but he could not blow the house in!

Said the wolf, "I shall come down the chimney."

"Come ahead!" said the third little pig as he uncovered a big pot of water that was boiling on the fire.

The big bad wolf came down the chimney and landed right in the pot of boiling water. With a yelp of pain he sprang straight up the chimney again and raced into the woods. The three little pigs never saw the big bad wolf again, and they spent the rest of their days in the strong little brick house, singing and dancing merrily.

Hansel and Gretel

Once upon a time there lived a poor woodcutter, his wife, and his two children, Hansel and Gretel. The wife was the children's stepmother, and she was very cruel to them.

One day the woodcutter said to his wife, "What shall we do? There is not enough food to feed us all."

"I have a plan," the stepmother said. "Early in the morning we will take the children into the forest and leave them there. They will never find their way home again."

The next morning, before the sun was up, the stepmother shouted to Hansel and Gretel, "Get up, you lazy children! We are going into the forest to cut wood. Here is a piece of bread. Don't eat it yet, because you won't get any more."

But Hansel and Gretel had heard what their stepmother had said to their father. As they walked deep into the forest Hansel left a trail of bread crumbs to help them find their way home.

When they reached the middle of the forest, the father built a fire. Then the stepmother said, "Wait here by the fire while we go to chop wood. We will come back to get you."

Hansel and Gretel knew they would not come back. The children tried to find the trail of bread crumbs, but birds had eaten them. They walked all day and night until the next morning.

Then they saw before them a little house, all made of gingerbread, with windows of spun sugar. The children ran to the house. Hansel ate a piece of roof and Gretel ate some windowpane. Suddenly they heard a voice.

"Nibble, nibble, like a mouse,
Who's that nibbling at my house?"

The door opened, and an old woman stepped out. "Do come in," she said sweetly. She fed Hansel and Gretel a wonderful dinner and put them to bed.

Now, although the old woman seemed very kind, she was really a wicked witch who ate little children.

The next morning she awakened Hansel and put him in a cage. Then she woke up Gretel and put her to work.

"I'm going to eat you both," she said. Each morning she asked Hansel to stick out his finger so she could feel how fat he was getting. At last she decided to eat him.

Gretel had to build the fire and fill the kettle. "Crawl in the oven and see if it is warm enough," said the witch.

"I don't know how," said Gretel. "You must show me."

So the old witch put her head in the oven. Quick as a flash, Gretel pushed her in and slammed the door! Then Gretel let Hansel out of his cage. "We're free!" they shouted. "The old witch is dead!"

They filled their pockets with glittering jewels from the witch's house. Then off they went to find their way home. Soon they heard a happy shout.

"Hansel! Gretel! I have searched and searched for you!" cried their father.

He took them home, and they all lived happily together, for their stepmother had gone away forever. And the money from the witch's jewels was more than enough for them to live well for the rest of their lives.

14.

Rumpelstiltskin

There once lived a miller who was so proud of his daughter's beauty that he boasted of it to everyone. One day the miller saw the king hunting in the forest.

"Sire," said the miller, "I have a daughter..."

"And I suppose she is very beautiful," said the king with a yawn.

"Oh, yes, she is beautiful!" said the miller. Before he could stop himself, he blurted, "And she can spin straw into gold!"

"Bring her to me at once!" ordered the king.

That evening the king led the miller's daughter into a little room. There was nothing in the room but a pile of straw, a spinning wheel, and a chair.

"Spin!" said the king. "Your father will be held prisoner until I have all the gold I need."

After the king left, the miller's daughter burst into tears because she did not really know how to spin straw into gold.

"Why do you weep?" asked a voice. The girl looked up and saw a little man.

"I must spin this straw into gold, and I don't know how," she said, sobbing.

"What will you give me if I do it for you?" the man asked.

"My necklace," said the girl. It was her most precious possession.

The little man took the necklace, and then he spun the straw into gold.

The next morning the king came in. He was very pleased to see all the gold, but he demanded that the girl make more. He left her with another pile of straw.

That night the little man appeared again before the weeping girl. This time the girl gave him her ring in exchange for his spinning.

The king came into the room the next morning. "You have done well," he said. But still more straw was brought into the room. "Spin this," the king said, "and tomorrow I will make you my wife."

After the king left, the little man came again. "What will you give me if I spin this into gold?"

"I have nothing left to give," said the girl sadly.

"Then you must promise me your firstborn child," said the little man.

"Anything you ask!" cried the girl.

The next morning the king was overcome with joy when he saw the shiny new gold.

"We shall be married at once!" he exclaimed. The miller's daughter became the queen, and a year later she had a beautiful baby daughter.

One evening the little man appeared to claim his reward.

"You may have everything I own," begged the queen, "but please don't take my baby!"

The little man said, "I will give you three days to find out my name. I will return each night for three nights. If you guess my name correctly, you may keep your child."

The queen sent messengers into the village to find the names of all the people there. The first night, when the little man returned, the queen told him all the names she could think of, but none was the right one. She failed the second evening as well.

On the third day one of the messengers came to the queen and said, "Deep in the forest, on the highest mountain, there lives an ugly little man. I put my ear to his window and this is what I heard:

> *'Today I brew, tomorrow I bake,*
> *The next day the queen's child I take.*
> *For the queen can never guess my fame—*
> *That Rumpelstiltskin is my name!'"*

"Rumpelstiltskin! That's it!" cried the queen.

When the little man came that night, he could hardly believe his ears.

"Someone told you!" he screamed in a rage. And he stamped so hard, he went right through the floor!

From that day on, the queen and her family lived happily ever after.

The Princess and the Pea

There once was a prince who wished to marry a real princess. He traveled the world far and wide searching for one. There were many who claimed to be princesses, but he could not be certain if they really were. He finally came home again and was quite sad, for he wished very much to have a real princess for his wife.

One night there was a terrible storm. It thundered, and the rain poured down. Then a knocking came at the gate of the town, and the old king went to open it.

It was a princess who stood outside the gate. But she was in a terrible state! The water ran down from her hair and her clothes, into the toes of her shoes, and out the heels. But she said she was a real princess.

"Well, that we shall soon find out," thought the old queen. She said nothing and went into the bedroom. After taking everything off the bed, she laid down a small pea, over which she heaped twenty mattresses, and then twenty quilts over them.

There the princess was to sleep that night.

In the morning the queen asked the princess how she had slept.

"Oh, terribly!" the princess answered. "I scarcely closed my eyes the whole night. Heaven knows what there may have been in the bed, but I lay upon something so hard that I am bruised all over."

It was evident, then, that she was a real princess, since she had felt the pea through the twenty mattresses and quilts. No one but a real princess could have such a fine sense of feeling.

So the prince married her, and the pea was placed in the royal museum, where it may still be seen.

Little Red Riding Hood

Once there was a little girl who lived with her mother in a house at the edge of the forest. The little girl was called Little Red Riding Hood because she always wore a red cloak and hood that her grandmother had made for her.

One day Little Red Riding Hood's mother said to her, "Grandmother is not feeling well. Please bring her this basket of fruit and cakes and honey, and be certain not to stop along the way."

"Yes, Mother," said Little Red Riding Hood.

Little Red Riding Hood had gone but a short way into the forest when a big gray wolf stepped out from behind a tree.

"Good morning, Little Red Riding Hood," said the wolf. "Where are you going on this fine day?"

"I'm going to see my grandmother. She is ill," said Little Red Riding Hood.

The wolf grinned to himself. "What a tasty treat this girl will make!" he thought greedily. "And the grandmother, too! This is my lucky day!"

"Why don't you pick some of these flowers for her?" he asked slyly.

"What a wonderful idea!" said Little Red Riding Hood. And so while she was busy picking flowers, the wolf ran ahead to Grandmother's house as fast as his legs would take him.

As soon as the wolf was inside, he bounded over to the bed and gobbled up Grandmother whole!

The wolf put on Grandmother's shawl and nightcap, and he crawled into bed to wait for Little Red Riding Hood.

"What big ears you have, Grandmother!" said Little Red Riding Hood when she finally arrived at Grandmother's house.

"The better to hear you with, my dear," said the wolf.

"And, Grandmother," said Little Red Riding Hood, "what big eyes you have!"

"The better to see you with, my dear," said the wolf. "Come closer, my child."

Little Red Riding Hood came closer. "Oh, Grandmother!" she said. "What big teeth you have!"

"The better to eat you with!" roared the wolf, and he grabbed Little Red Riding Hood and gobbled her up whole!

Then, feeling full and satisfied, the wolf lay down and fell asleep.

Now, it happened that a woodcutter was passing Grandmother's cottage just at that moment. He knew Grandmother had not been feeling well, so he decided to check in on her.

When the woodcutter saw the wolf snoring on the bed, he knew at once what had happened.

"I have you at last, you devil," he said, and he slew the wolf with his ax. Then the woodcutter took a carving knife and carefully slit open the wolf's belly. Out popped Little Red Riding Hood and her grandmother, safe and whole.

Little Red Riding Hood, Grandmother, and the woodcutter sat down to feast on fruit and cakes and honey. And they all lived happily ever after and were never troubled with the evil wolf again.

24.

Rapunzel

Once upon a time there lived a husband and wife who were very sad because they had no children.

One day the woman sat staring through her window at her neighbor's vegetable garden.

"If I don't get some of that lettuce soon, I will simply die!" she said.

Now, the husband loved his wife with all his heart, so he did exactly as his wife asked.

"If you want lettuce, you must pay for it!" cackled a voice in the garden. "The pay I demand for my lettuce is this: When a child is born to your wife, it shall be mine!"

25.

The husband realized that this woman was indeed a witch. But since he was certain he and his wife would never have a child, he said, "Very well."

It just so happened that the couple did have a child—a lovely little girl they called Rapunzel. And soon after her birth, the witch appeared at their door.

"Give me your baby, or I will cast a spell on her!"

So Rapunzel went to live with the witch in her home in the forest. She grew to be quite beautiful, and she had very long golden hair.

26.

When Rapunzel was twelve years old, the witch locked her up in a little room at the top of a tower. The only way to reach her was through a window. When the witch wanted to visit her, she would call out, "Rapunzel, Rapunzel, let down your hair." Then the witch would climb up Rapunzel's braid to the window and into the tower room.

Several years had passed when one day a handsome prince who was riding in the woods heard the witch call to Rapunzel. Then he watched as the old witch climbed up her braid to the tower. As soon as he caught sight of Rapunzel, he fell in love with her.

The next day the prince returned to the tower. Just as the witch had done, he called out to Rapunzel and climbed up her braid to meet her. When Rapunzel saw the prince, she fell in love with him. But neither of them knew that the witch had seen everything.

The next day the witch grabbed Rapunzel and cut off her golden braid. Then she took Rapunzel away and left her alone, deep in the forest.

Later, when the prince called out to Rapunzel, the witch wrapped the braid around a hook and let it down to him. The prince climbed up and was shocked to see the witch there instead of Rapunzel.

"I will share Rapunzel with no one!" the witch shrieked. "You will never see her again. She is gone forever!"

The prince was so brokenhearted that he jumped out of the window. He fell among thorns, which scratched his eyes and made him blind.

Two years passed. Rapunzel lived miserably, having only berries and roots to eat. The prince wandered blindly through the land, unable to find his way home.

Then one day Rapunzel saw a poor, ragged-looking man. It was the prince! Rapunzel recognized him instantly. She threw her arms around him and wept for joy. Two of her tears fell on his eyes, and they were healed. The prince could see again!

And so the prince took Rapunzel to his palace. They were married there before the entire kingdom, and they lived happily ever after.

28.